IMPLEMENTS IN THEIR PLACES

THE NIGHTFISHING (1955)
THE WHITE THRESHOLD (1949)
MALCOLM MOONEY'S LAND (1970)

CAGE WITHOUT GRIEVANCE (1942)
(*Parton Press, David Archer*)
THE SEVEN JOURNEYS (1944)
(*McLellan, Glasgow*)
2ND POEMS (1945)
(*Nicholson and Watson*)

IMPLEMENTS
IN THEIR PLACES

W. S. Graham

FABER & FABER
3 QUEEN SQUARE
LONDON

First published in 1977
by Faber and Faber Limited
3 Queen Square London WC1
Printed in Great Britain by
Latimer Trend & Company Ltd Plymouth
All rights reserved

British Library Cataloguing in Publication Data

Graham, William Sydney
Implements in their places.
I. Title
821'.9'14   PR6013.RZ3

ISBN 0-571-10955-1

EXCEPT NESSIE DUNSMUIR

Acknowledgements

Acknowledgements are due to the following periodicals in which some of these poems earlier appeared:

The Listener, Malahat Review, New Poems 1975, Akros, Poetry Nation, P.N Review, The Times Literary Supplement, Pembroke Magazine, Aquarius, Stand, The London Magazine, Cracked Looking Glass.

The author wishes to thank The Arts Council for a grant in the summer of 1975.

Contents

WHAT IS THE LANGUAGE USING US FOR?

First Poem

What is the language using us for?
Said Malcolm Mooney moving away
Slowly over the white language.
Where am I going said Malcolm Mooney.

Certain experiences seem to not
Want to go in to language maybe
Because of shame or the reader's shame.
Let us observe Malcolm Mooney.

Let us get through the suburbs and drive
Out further just for fun to see
What he will do. Reader, it does
Not matter. He is only going to be

Myself and for you slightly you
Wanting to be another. He fell
He falls (Tenses are everywhere.)
Deep down into a glass jail.

I am in a telephoneless, blue
Green crevasse and I can't get out.
I pay well for my messages
Being hoisted up when you are about.

I suppose you open them under the light
Of midnight of The Dancing Men.
The point is would you ever want
To be down here on the freezing line

Reading the words that steam out
Against the ice? Anyhow draw
This folded message up between
The leaning prisms from me below.

Slowly over the white language
Comes Malcolm Mooney the saviour.
My left leg has no feeling.
What is the language using us for?

Second Poem

I

What is the language using us for?
It uses us all and in its dark
Of dark actions selections differ.

I am not making a fool of myself
For you. What I am making is
A place for language in my life

Which I want to be a real place
Seeing I have to put up with it
Anyhow. What are Communication's

Mistakes in the magic medium doing
To us? It matters only in
So far as we want to be telling

Each other alive about each other
Alive. I want to be able to speak
And sing and make my soul occur

In front of the best and be respected
For that and even be understood
By the ones I like who are dead.

I would like to speak in front
Of myself with all my ears alive
And find out what it is I want.

2

What is the language using us for?
What shape of words shall put its arms
Round us for more than pleasure?

I met a man in Cartsburn Street
Thrown out of the Cartsburn Vaults.
He shouted Willie and I crossed the street

And met him at the mouth of the Close.
And this was double-breasted Sam,
A far relation on my mother's

West-Irish side. Hello Sam how
Was it you knew me and says he
I heard your voice on The Sweet Brown Knowe.

O was I now I said and Sam said
Maggie would have liked to see you.
I'll see you again I said and said

Sam I'll not keep you and turned
Away over the shortcut across
The midnight railway sidings.

What is the language using us for?
From the prevailing weather or words
Each object hides in a metaphor.

This is the morning. I am out
On a kind of Vlaminck blue-rutted
Road. Willie Wagtail is about.

In from the West a fine smirr
Of rain drifts across the hedge.
I am only out here to walk or

Make this poem up. The hill is
A shining blue macadam top.
I lean my back to the telegraph pole

And the messages hum through my spine.
The beaded wires with their birds
Above me are contacting London.

What is the language using us for?
It uses us all and in its dark
Of dark actions selections differ.

Third Poem

I

What is the language using us for?
The King of Whales dearly wanted
To have a word with me about how
I had behaved trying to crash
The Great Barrier. I could not speak
Or answer him easily in the white
Crystal of Art he set me in.

Who is the King of Whales? What is
He like? Well you may ask. He is
A kind of old uncle of mine
And yours mushing across the blind
Ice-cap between us in his furs
Shouting at his delinquent dogs.
What is his purpose? I try to find

14

Whatever it is is wanted by going
Out of my habits which is my name
To ask him how I can do better.
Tipped from a cake of ice I slid
Into the walrus-barking water
To find. I did not find another
At the end of my cold cry.

2

What is the language using us for?
The sailing men had sailing terms
Which rigged their inner-sailing thoughts
In forecastle and at home among
The kitchen of their kind. Tarry
Old Jack is taken aback at a blow
On the lubber of his domestic sea.

Sam, I had thought of going again
But it's no life. I signed on years
Ago and it wasn't the ship for me.
O leave 'er Johnny leave 'er.
Sam, what readers do we have aboard?
Only the one, Sir. Who is that?
Only myself, Sir, from Cartsburn Street.

3

What is the language using us for?
I don't know. Have the words ever
Made anything of you, near a kind
Of truth you thought you were? Me
Neither. The words like albatrosses
Are only a doubtful touch towards
My going and you lifting your hand

To speak to illustrate an observed
Catastrophe. What is the weather
Using us for where we are ready
With all our language lines aboard?
The beginning wind slaps the canvas.
Are you ready? Are you ready?

IMAGINE A FOREST

Imagine a forest
A real forest.

You are walking in it and it sighs
Round you where you go in a deep
Ballad on the border of a time
You have seemed to walk in before.
It is nightfall and you go through
Trying to find between the twittering
Shades the early starlight edge
Of the open moor land you know.
I have set you here and it is not a dream
I put you through. Go on between
The elephant bark of those beeches
Into that lightening, almost glade.

And he has taken
My word and gone

Through his own Ettrick darkening
Upon himself and he's come across
A glinted knight lying dying
On needles under a high tree.
Ease his visor open gently
To reveal whatever white, encased
Face will ask out at you who
It is you are or if you will
Finish him off. His eyes are open.
Imagine he does not speak. Only
His beard moving against the metal
Signs that he would like to speak.

Imagine a room
Where you are home

Taking your boots off from the wood
In that deep ballad very not
A dream and the fire noisily
Kindling up and breaking its sticks.
Do not imagine I put you there
For nothing. I put you through it
There in that holt of words between
The bearded liveoaks and the beeches
For you to meet a man alone
Slipping out of whatever cause
He thought he lay there dying for.

Hang up the ballad
Behind the door.

You are come home but you are about
To not fight hard enough and die
In a no less desolate dark wood
Where a stranger shall never enter.

Imagine a forest
A real forest.

UNTIDY DREADFUL TABLE

Lying with no love on the paper
Between the typing hammers I spied
Myself with looking eyes looking
Down to cover me with words.

I won't have it. I know the night
Is late here sitting at my table,
But I am not a boy running
The hide and seeking streets.

I am getting on. My table now
Shuffles its papers out of reach
With last year's letters going yellow
From looking out of the window.

I sit here late and I hammer myself
On to the other side of the paper.
There I jump through all surprises.
The reader and I are making faces.

I am not complaining. Some of the faces
I see are interesting indeed.
Take your own, for example, a fine
Grimace of vessels over the bone.

Of course I see you backwards covered
With words backwards from the other side.
I must tackle my dreadful table
And go on the hide and seeking hill.

A NOTE TO THE DIFFICULT ONE

This morning I am ready if you are,
To hear you speaking in your new language.
I think I am beginning to have nearly
A way of writing down what it is I think
You say. You enunciate very clearly
Terrible words always just beyond me.

I stand in my vocabulary looking out
Through my window of fine water ready
To translate natural occurrences
Into something beyond any idea
Of pleasure. The wisps of April fly
With light messages to the lonely.

This morning I am ready if you are
To speak. The early quick rains
Of Spring are drenching the window-glass.
Here in my words looking out
I see your face speaking flying
In a cloud wanting to say something.

ARE YOU STILL THERE?

I love I love you tucked away
In a corner of my time looking
Out at me for me to put
My arm round you to comfort you.

I love you more than that as well
You know. You know I live now
In Madron with the black, perched beasts
On the shoulder of the gable-end.

The first day of October's bright
Shadows go over the Celtic fields
Coming to see you. I have tucked
You I hope not too far away.

LANGUAGE AH NOW YOU HAVE ME

I

Language ah now you have me. Night-time tongue,
Please speak for me between the social beasts
Which quick assail me. Here I am hiding in
The jungle of mistakes of communication.

I know about jungles. I know about unkempt places
Flying toward me when I am getting ready
To pull myself together and plot the place
To speak from. I am at the jungle face
Which is not easily yours. It is my home
Where pigmies hamstring Jumbo and the pleasure
Monkey is plucked from the tree. How pleased I am
To meet you reading and writing on damp paper
In the rain forest beside the Madron River.

2

Which is my home. The great and small breathers,
Experts of speaking, hang and slowly move
To say something or spring in the steaming air
Down to do the great white hunter for ever.

3

Do not disturb me now. I have to extract
A creature with its eggs between the words.
I have to seize it now, otherwise not only
My vanity will be appalled but my good cat
Will not look at me in the same way.

4

Is not to look. We are the ones hanging
On here and there, the dear word's edge wondering
If we are speaking clearly enough or if
The jungle's acoustics are at fault. Baboon,
My soul, is always ready to relinquish
The safe hold and leap on to nothing at all.
At least I hope so. Language now you have me
Trying to be myself but changed into
The wildebeest pursued or the leo pard
Running at stretch beside the Madron River.

5

Too much. I died. I forgot who I was and sent
My heart back with my bearers. How pleased I am
To find you here beside the Madron River
Wanting to be spoken to. It is my home
Where pigmies hamstring Jumbo and the pleasure
Monkey is plucked from the tree.

TWO POEMS ON ZENNOR HILL

1

Ancient of runes the stone-cut voice
Stands invisible on Zennor Hill.
I climb here in a morning of mist
Up over a fox's or badger's track
And there is no sound but myself
Breaking last year's drenched bracken.

2

O foxglove on the wall
You meet me nicely today
Leaning your digitalis
Bells toward the house
Bryan Wynterless.

I stand on the high Zennor
Moor with lint and sour
Grass and the loose stone walls
Keeping the weasel's castle.
O foxglove on the wall.

TEN SHOTS OF MISTER SIMPSON

1

Ah Mister Simpson shy spectator
This morning in our November,
Don't run away with the idea
You are you spectating me.

On the contrary from this hide
Under my black cloth I see
You through the lens close enough
For comfort. Yes slightly turn

Your head more to the right and don't
Don't blink your eyes against the rain.
I have I almost have you now.
I want the line of the sea in.

Now I have you too close up.
As a face your face has disappeared.
All I see from my black tent
Is on the shelf of your lower lid
A tear like a travelling rat.

2

The camera nudges him to scream
Silently into its face.
Silently his thought recalls
Across the side of Zennor Hill.

He is here only recalling
Himself being pointed at

By somebody ago and even not
Understanding the language.

I am to do him no harm.
Mister Simpson, stand still.
Look at him standing sillily
For our sake and for the sake
Of preservation. He imagines
Still he is going to be shot.

3

He is as real as you looking
Over my November shoulder.
The sky chimes and the slewing light
Comes over Zennor Hill striking
The white of his escaped head.
His face comes dazzling through the glass
Into my eye imprisoned by Art.
His wife is gone. He has a daughter
Somewhere. Shall I snap him now?
No, you take him and get the number
Now that he's rolled up his sleeves.

4

Mister Simpson Blakean bright
Exile in our Sunday morning,
Stand still get ready jump in your place
Lie down get up don't speak. Number?
Fear not. It is only the high Zennor
Kestrel and I have clicked the shutter.

This time I want your face trying
To not remember dear other
Numbers you left, who did not follow
Follow follow you into this kind
Of last home held below the Zennor
Bracken fires and hovering eye.
Move and turn your unpronounceable
Name's head to look at where the horse
Black in its meadow noses the stone.

And here I am today below
The hill invisible in mist
In impossible light knocking.
My subject does not expect me.

Mister Simpson, can I with my drenched
Eyes but not with weeping come in?
Five diminishing tureens hang
Answering the fire from the kitchen wall.
There is a dog lying with cataracting
Eyes under a table. The mantel's brasses
Makes a bright gloom and in the corner
A narrow Kiev light makes an ikon.

And who would have it in verse but only
Yourself too near having come in only
To look over my shoulder to see
How it is done. You are wrong. You are wrong
Being here, but necessary. Somebody
Else must try to see what I see.

Mister Simpson, turn your face
To get the gold of the fire on it.

Keep still. I have you nearly now.

So I made that. I got in also
A His Master's Voice gramophone,
A jug of Sheepsbit Scabious and
A white-rigged ship bottled sailing
And the mantel-piece in focus with even
A photograph of five young gassed
Nephews and nieces fading brown.

7

Not a cloud, the early wide morning
Has us both in, me looking
And you looking. Come and stand.
Aloft the carn behind you moves
So slowly down to anciently
Remember men looking at men
As uneasily as us. Mister Simpson,
Forgive me. The whole high moor is moving
Down to keep us safe in its gaze
As looking-at-each-other beasts
Who suddenly fly running into
The lens from fearful, opposite sides.
Not a cloud, the early wide morning
Has us both in looking out.

8

Mister Simpson, kneedeep in the drowned
Thistles of not your own country,
What is your category? What number
Did you curl into alone to sleep
The cold away in Hut K
Fifty-five nearest God the Chimney?

Now I have you sighted far
Out of the blackthorn and the wired
Perimeter into this particular
No less imprisoned place. You shall
Emerge here within different
Encirclements in a different time
Where I can ask you to lean easily
Against the young ash at your door
And with your hand touch your face
And look through into my face and into
The gentle reader's deadly face.

9

Today below this buzzard hill
Of real weather manufactured
By me the wisps slide slowly
Over the cottage you stand courageously
Outside of with a spade in your hand.
Pretend the mist has come across
Straight from your own childhood gathering
Berries on a picnic. The mist
Is only yours, I see by your face.
I am charging you nothing, Mister
Simpson. Stand and look easily
Beyond me as you always do.
I have you now and you didn't even
Feel anything but I have killed you.

10

Ah Mister Simpson shy spectator
This morning in our November,
I focus us across the curving
World's edge to put us down
For each other into the ordinary
Weather to be seen together still.

Language, put us down for the last
Time under real Zennor Hill
Before it moves into cloud.

Ah Mister Simpson, Ah Reader, Ah
Myself, our pictures are being taken.
We stand still. Zennor Hill,
Language and light begin to go
To leave us looking at each other.

THE NIGHT CITY

Unmet at Euston in a dream
Of London under Turner's steam
Misting the iron gantries, I
Found myself running away
From Scotland into the golden city.

I ran down Gray's Inn Road and ran
Till I was under a black bridge.
This was me at nineteen
Late at night arriving between
The buildings of the City of London.

And then I (O I have fallen down)
Fell in my dream beside the Bank
Of England's wall to bed, me
With my money belt of Northern ice.
I found Eliot and he said yes

And sprang into a Holmes cab.
Boswell passed me in the fog
Going to visit Whistler who
Was with John Donne who had just seen
Paul Potts shouting on Soho Green.

Midnight. I hear the moon
Light chiming on St Paul's.

The City is empty. Night
Watchmen are drinking their tea.

The Fire had burnt out.
The Plague's pits had closed
And gone into literature.

Between the big buildings
I sat like a flea crouched
In the stopped works of a watch.

ENTER A CLOUD

Gently disintegrate me
Said nothing at all.

Is there still time to say
Said I myself lying
In a bower of bramble
Into which I have fallen.

Look through my eyes up
At blue with not anything
We could have ever arranged
Slowly taking place.

Above the spires of the fox
Gloves and above the bracken
Tops with their young heads
Recognising the wind,
The armies of the empty
Blue press me further
Into Zennor Hill.

If I half-close my eyes
The spiked light leaps in
And I am here as near
Happy as I will get
In the sailing afternoon.

Enter a cloud. Between
The head of Zennor and
Gurnard's Head the long
Marine horizon makes
A blue wall or is it
A distant table-top
Of the far-off simple sea.

Enter a cloud. O cloud,
I see you entering from
Your west gathering yourself
Together into a white
Headlong. And now you move
And stream out of the Gurnard,
The west corner of my eye.

Enter a cloud. The cloud's
Changing shape is crossing
Slowly only an inch
Above the line of the sea.
Now nearly equidistant
Between Zennor and Gurnard's
Head, an elongated
White anvil is sailing
Not wanting to be a symbol.

3

Said nothing at all.

And proceeds with no idea
Of destination along
The sea bearing changing
Messages. Jean in London,

Lifting a cup, looking
Abstractedly out through
Her Hampstead glass will never
Be caught by your new shape
Above the chimneys. Jean,
Jean, do you not see
This cloud has been thought of
And written on Zennor Hill.

4

The cloud is going beyond
What I can see or make.
Over up-country maybe
Albert Strick stops and waves
Caught in the middle of teeling
Broccoli for the winter.
The cloud is not there yet.

From Gurnard's Head To Zennor
Head the level line
Crosses my eyes lying
On buzzing Zennor Hill.

The cloud is only a wisp
And gone behind the Head.
It is funny I got the sea's
Horizontal slightly surrealist.
Now when I raise myself
Out of the bracken I see
The long empty blue
Between the fishing Gurnard
And Zennor. It was a cloud
The language at my time's
Disposal made use of.

Thank you. And for your applause.
It has been a pleasure. I
Have never enjoyed speaking more.
May I also thank the real ones
Who have made this possible.
First, the cloud itself. And now
Gurnard's Head and Zennor
Head. Also recognise
How I have been helped
By Jean and Madron's Albert
Strick (He is a real man.)
And good words like brambles,
Bower, spiked, fox, anvil, teeling.

The bees you heard are from
A hive owned by my friend
Garfield down there below
In the house by Zennor Church.

The good blue sun is pressing
Me into Zennor Hill.

Gently disintegrate me
Said nothing at all.

GREENOCK AT NIGHT I FIND YOU

I

As for you loud Greenock long ropeworking
Hide and seeking rivetting town of my child
Hood, I know we think of us often mostly
At night. Have you ever desired me back
Into the set-in bed at the top of the land
In One Hope Street? I am myself lying
Half-asleep hearing the rivetting yards
And smelling the bone-works with no home
Work done for Cartsburn School in the morning.

At night. And here I am descending and
The welding lights in the shipyards flower blue
Under my hopeless eyelids as I lie
Sleeping conditioned to hide from happy.

2

So what did I do? I walked from Hope Street
Down Lyndoch Street between the night's words
To Cartsburn Street and got to the Cartsburn Vaults
With half an hour to go. See, I am back.

3

See, I am back. My father turned and I saw
He had the stick he cut in Sheelhill Glen.
Brigit was there and Hugh and double-breasted
Sam and Malcolm Mooney and Alastair Graham.
They all were there in the Cartsburn Vaults shining
To meet me but I was only remembered.

LOCH THOM

Just for the sake of recovering
I walked backward from fifty-six
Quick years of age wanting to see,
And managed not to trip or stumble
To find Loch Thom and turned round
To see the stretch of my childhood
Before me. Here is the loch. The same
Long-beaked cry curls across
The heather-edges of the water held
Between the hills a boyhood's walk
Up from Greenock. It is the morning.

And I am here with my mammy's
Bramble-jam scones in my pocket.
The Firth is miles and I have come
Back to find Loch Thom maybe
In this light does not recognise me.

This is a lonely freshwater loch.
No farms on the edge. Only
Heather grouse-moor stretching
Down to Greenock and One Hope
Street or stretching away across
Into the blue moors of Ayrshire.

2

And almost I am back again
Wading the heather down to the edge

To sit. The minnows go by in shoals
Like iron-filings in the shallows.

My mother is dead. My father is dead
And all the trout I used to know
Leaping from their sad rings are dead.

3

I drop my crumbs into the shallow
Weed for the minnows and pinheads.
You see that I will have to rise
And turn round and get back where
My running age will slow for a moment
To let me on. It is a colder
Stretch of water than I remember.

The curlew's cry travelling still
Kills me fairly. In front of me
The grouse flurry and settle. GOBACK
GOBACK GOBACK FAREWELL LOCH THOM.

TO ALEXANDER GRAHAM

Lying asleep walking
Last night I met my father
Who seemed pleased to see me.
He wanted to speak. I saw
His mouth saying something
But the dream had no sound.

We were surrounded by
Laid-up paddle steamers
In The Old Quay in Greenock.
I smelt the tar and the ropes.

It seemed that I was standing
Beside the big iron cannon
The tugs used to tie up to
When I was a boy. I turned
To see Dad standing just
Across the causeway under
That one lamp they keep on.

He recognised me immediately.
I could see that. He was
The handsome, same age
With his good brows as when
He would take me on Sundays
Saying we'll go for a walk.

Dad, what am I doing here?
What is it I am doing now?
Are you proud of me?
Going away, I knew
You wanted to tell me something.

You stopped and almost turned back
To say something. My father,
I try to be the best
In you you give me always.

Lying asleep turning
Round in the quay-lit dark
It was my father standing
As real as life. I smelt
The quay's tar and the ropes.

I think he wanted to speak.
But the dream had no sound.
I think I must have loved him.

SGURR NA GILLEAN MACLEOD

(For the Makar & Childer)

Dear Makar Norman, here's a letter
Riming nearly to the Scots bone.
I rime it for it helps the thought
To sail across and makes the thought
  Into your Leod heid fly.
I thought I saw your words going
  Over the sea to Skye.

Here I speak from the first of light
On Loch Coruisk's crying shore.
Each bare foot prints the oystercatching
Sand and the ebb is cold streaming
  Itself and creatures by
Between my whole ten toes singing
  Over the sea to Skye.

Norman, you could probably make
This poem better than I can.
Except you are not here. Roll up
Your trews and let the old loch lap
  Your shanks of Poetry.
The bladder-wrack is smelling us
  Over the sea to Skye.

Maybe it doesn't matter what
The poem is doing on its own.
But yet I am a man who rows
This light skiff of words across
  Silence's far cry.
Don't be misled by rime. I row you
  Over the sea to Skye.

Norman, Skye, Norman I shout
Across the early morning loch.
Can you hear me from where I am?
Out on the shining Gaelic calm
  I hear your three names fly.
Look. It is the birds of Macleod
   Over the sea to Skye.

I row. I dip my waterbright blades
Into the loch and into silence
And pull and feather my oars and bright
Beads of the used water of light
  Drip off astern to die
And mix with the little whirling pools
   Over the sea to Skye.

And I am rowing the three of you
Far out now. Norman and Skye
And Norman keep the good skiff trim.
Don't look back where we are going from.
  Sailing these words we fly
Out into the ghost-waved open sea
   Over the sea to Skye.

PRIVATE POEM TO NORMAN MACLEOD

I

Norman, the same wind
Of gannets and the malt
Whisky is blowing over
To how you are there
In North Carolina.

I hope it brings you a wisp
Of me sitting here
At my writing table.
Do you think we could get on
After that long time
In New York years and years
Ago when Vivienne was alive?

I see you now through
The early Madron morning
With rooks speaking Cornish
And getting into a high
Discussion above Strick's
Trees. My dear Norman,
I don't think we will ever
See each other again
Except through the spaces
We make occur between
The words to each other.

Now your trip is over
And you are back at home.
Of course, here I am
Thinking I want to say

Something into the ghost
Of the presence you have left
Me with between the granite
Of my ego house.

Your visit was a great
Occasion. It is with me now.
I'll always remember you.

2

Early wading on the long
Strand with oyster-catchers
Going peep-peep I looked
Up at the Gaelic Ross
To see a gigantic American
Out of all proportion
Standing against the west
Of Skye making his memoirs
After making his poetry
And genius editing. I
Waded through the Atlantic
Kelp washed up by the west.

And here I stand and I
Would dearly like to have spoken
To Norman Macleod but the gales
That blow in the memory
Change everything round.
I speak from myself now.

3

Macleod. Macleod. The white
Pony of your Zodiac
Trots down here often.

I look at him. He is only
A thought out of a book
You younger made. He's far
Trotted out of his home.
That distance from your boyhood
He nuzzles. Good boy. Good boy.

And after you went back
I thought I could have behaved
Better or was it you.
But it doesn't work like that.

4

Communication is always
On the edge of ridiculous.
Nothing on that, my Beauty.
I walked up Fouste Canyon
With a pack of beans and malt
Whisky and climbed and shouted
Norman   Norman   Norman
Till all the echoes had gone.

In the words there is always
A great greedy space
Ready to engulf the traveller.

Norman, you were not there.

5

Remember the title. A PRIVATE
POEM TO NORMAN MACLEOD.
But this, my boy, is the poem
You paid me five pounds for.
The idea of me making

Those words fly together
In seemingly a private
Letter is just me choosing
An attitude to make a poem.

6

Pembroke gentle and un
Gentle readers, this poem
Is private with me speaking
To Norman Macleod, as private
As any poem is private
With spaces between the words.
The spaces in the poem are yours.
They are the place where you
Can enter as yourself alone
And think anything in.
Macleod. Macleod, say
Hello before we both
Go down the manhole.

JOHANN JOACHIM QUANTZ'S FIVE LESSONS

The First Lesson

So that each person may quickly find that
Which particularly concerns him, certain metaphors
Convenient to us within the compass of this
Lesson are to be allowed. It is best I sit
Here where I am to speak on the other side
Of language. You, of course, in your own time
And incident (I speak in the small hours.)
Will listen from your side. I am very pleased
We have sought us out. No doubt you have read
My Flute Book. Come. The Guild clock's iron men
Are striking out their few deserted hours
And here from my high window Brueghel's winter
Locks the canal below. I blow my fingers.

The Second Lesson

Good morning, Karl. Sit down. I have been thinking
About your progress and my progress as one
Who teaches you, a young man with talent
And the rarer gift of application. I think
You must now be becoming a musician
Of a certain calibre. It is right maybe
That in our lessons now I should expect
Slight and very polite impatiences
To show in you. Karl, I think it is true,
You are now nearly able to play the flute.

Now we must try higher, aware of the terrible
Shapes of silence sitting outside your ear

Anxious to define you and really love you.
Remember silence is curious about its opposite
Element which you shall learn to represent.

Enough of that. Now stand in the correct position
So that the wood of the floor will come up through you.
Stand, but not too stiff. Keep your elbows down.
Now take a simple breath and make me a shape
Of clear unchained started and finished tones.
Karl, as well as you are able, stop
Your fingers into the breathing apertures
And speak and make the cylinder delight us.

The Third Lesson

Karl, you are late. The traverse flute is not
A study to take lightly. I am cold waiting.
Put one piece of coal in the stove. This lesson
Shall not be prolonged. Right. Stand in your place.

Ready? Blow me a little ladder of sound
From a good stance so that you feel the heavy
Press of the floor coming up through you and
Keeping your pitch and tone in character.

Now that is something, Karl. You are getting on.
Unswell your head. One more piece of coal.
Go on now but remember it must be always
Easy and flowing. Light and shadow must
Be varied but be varied in your mind
Before you hear the eventual return sound.

Play me the dance you made for the barge-master.
Stop stop Karl. Play it as you first thought
Of it in the hot boat-kitchen. That is a pleasure
For me. I can see I am making you good.
Keep the stove red. Hand me the matches. Now

We can see better. Give me a shot at the pipe.
Karl, I can still put on a good flute-mouth
And show you in this high cold room something
You will be famous to have said you heard.

The Fourth Lesson

You are early this morning. What we have to do
Today is think of you as a little creator
After the big creator. And it can be argued
You are as necessary, even a composer
Composing in the flesh an attitude
To slay the ears of the gentry. Karl,
I know you find great joy in the great
Composers. But now you can put your lips to
The messages and blow them into sound
And enter and be there as well. You must
Be faithful to who you are speaking from
And yet it is all right. You will be there.

Take your coat off. Sit down. A glass of Bols
Will help us both. I think you are good enough
To not need me anymore. I think you know
You are not only an interpreter.
What you will do is always something else
And they will hear you simultaneously with
The Art you have been given to read. Karl,

I think the Spring is really coming at last.
I see the canal boys working. I realise
I have not asked you to play the flute today.
Come and look. Are the barges not moving?
You must forgive me. I am not myself today.
Be here on Thursday. When you come, bring
Me five herrings. Watch your fingers. Spring
Is apparent but it is still chilblain weather.

The Last Lesson

Dear Karl, this morning is our last lesson.
I have been given the opportunity to
Live in a certain person's house and tutor
Him and his daughters on the traverse flute.
Karl, you will be all right. In those recent
Lessons my heart lifted to your playing.

I know. I see you doing well, invited
In a great chamber in front of the gentry. I
Can see them with their dresses settling in
And bored mouths beneath moustaches sizing
You up as you are, a lout from the canal
With big ears but an angel's tread on the flute.

But you will be all right. Stand in your place
Before them. Remember Johann. Begin with good
Nerve and decision. Do not intrude too much
Into the message you carry and put out.

One last thing, Karl, remember when you enter
The joy of those quick high archipelagoes,
To make to keep your finger-stops as light
As feathers but definite. What can I say more?
Do not be sentimental or in your Art.
I will miss you. Do not expect applause.

THE GOBBLED CHILD

To set the scene. It is April
Early with little streams
Of tide running out
Between the kelp and bladders
On the still loch-side.

From the big house behind us
Five-year-old Iain
Comes out to play under
The mewing of terns
And peeping oystercatchers.

His father is up and out
Driving his loud, begulled
Tractor on the high field.
Maggy hums on the green
With a clothes-peg in her teeth.

And Iain with his fair head
Cocked stands listening
To a magic, held shell
And a big beast comes out
Of the loch and gobbles him up.

To set the scene. It is April
Early with little streams
Of tide running out
Between the kelp and bladders
On the still loch-side.

THE LOST MISS CONN

To set the scene. The kirk
Helpers and two elders
Are clearing up from the fête.
Wasps are at the jam.
Miss Conn is going home.

She scorns young MacIvor
And trips into the wood.
Hazel and oak and rowan.
It is not a dark wood
Like the Black Wood of Madron.

Yellow-beak and the jay
Make a happy noise round
Where she treads. She treads
Her way budding gently
Unhappy for MacIvor.

So she was seen to enter
The wood with her young skirt
Flashing. Mr & Mrs
Conn never received her.
Hazel and oak and rowan.

To set the scene. The kirk
Helpers and two elders
Are clearing up from the fête.
Wasps are at the jam.
Miss Conn is going home.

THE MURDERED DRINKER

To set the scene. The night
Wind is rushing the moon
Across the winter road.
A mile away a farm
Blinks its oily eye.

Inside snug MacLellan's
Old Rab, the earth's salt,
Knocks one back for the road.
The pub collie lifts
Its nose as he slams the door.

Rab takes the road. The oak
Wood on his left is flying
Away into itself.
At his right hand the big
Branches of elm flail.

By Rhue Corner he stops
And leans on the buzzing pole
And undeservedly
A sick bough of the storm
Falls and murders him.

To set the scene. The night
Wind is rushing the moon
Across the winter road.
A mile away a farm
Blinks its oily eye.

HOW ARE THE CHILDREN ROBIN

(FOR ROBIN SKELTON)

It does not matter how are you how are
The children flying leaving home so early?
The song is lost asleep the blackthorn breaks
Into its white flourish. The poet walks
At all odd times hoping the road is empty.
I mean me walking hoping the road is empty.

Not that I would ever expect to see
Them over the brow of the hill coming
In scarlet anoraks to meet their Dad.
A left, a right, my mad feet trudge the road
Between the busy times. It raineth now
Across the hedges and beneath the bough.

It does not matter let that be a lesson
To cross the fields. Keep off the road. The Black
Wood of Madron with its roof of rooks
Is lost asleep flying into the dusk.
When shall we see the children older returning
Into the treetops? And what are they bringing?

THE STEPPING STONES

I have my yellow boots on to walk
Across the shires where I hide
Away from my true people and all
I can't put easily into my life.

So you will see I am stepping on
The stones between the runnels getting
Nowhere nowhere. It is almost
Embarrassing to be alive alone.

Take my hand and pull me over from
The last stone on to the moss and
The three celandines. Now my dear
Let us go home across the shires.

LINES ON ROGER HILTON'S WATCH

Which I was given because
I loved him and we had
Terrible times together.

O tarnished ticking time
Piece with your bent hand,
You must be used to being
Looked at suddenly
In the middle of the night
When he switched the light on
Beside his bed. I hope
You told him the best time
When he lifted you up
To meet the Hilton gaze.

I lift you up from the mantel
Piece here in my house
Wearing your verdigris.
At least I keep you wound
And put my ear to you
To hear Botallack tick.

You realise your master
Has relinquished you
And gone to lie under
The ground at St Just.

Tell me the time. The time
Is Botallack o'clock.
This is the dead of night.

He switches the light on
To find a cigarette
And pours himself a Teachers.
He picks me up and holds me
Near his lonely face
To see my hands. He thinks
He is not being watched.

The images of his dream
Are still about his face
As he spits and tries not
To remember where he was.

I am only a watch
And pray time hastes away.
I think I am running down.

Watch, it is time I wound
You up again. I am
Very much not your dear
Last master but we had
Terrible times together.

THE SECRET NAME

1

Whatever you've come here to get
You've come to the wrong place. It
(I mean your name.) hurries away
Before you in the trees to escape.

I am against you looking in
At what you think is me speaking.
Yet we know I am not against
You looking at me and hearing.

If I had met you earlier walking
With the poetry light better
We might we could have spoken and said
Our names to each other. Under

Neath the boughs of the last black
Bird fluttered frightened in the shade
I think you might be listening. I
Listen in this listening wood.

To tell you the truth I hear almost
Only the sounds I have made myself.
Up over the wood's roof I imagine
The long sigh of Outside goes.

2

I leave them there for a moment knowing
I make them act you and me.

59

Under the poem's branches two people
Walk and even the words are shy.

It is only an ordinary wood.
It is the wood out of my window.
Look, the words are going away
Into it now like a black hole.

Five fields away Madron Wood
Is holding words and putting them.
I can hear them there. They move
As a darkness of my family.

3

The terrible, lightest wind in the world
Blows from word to word, from ear
To ear, from name to name, from secret
Name to secret name. You maybe
Did not know you had another
Sound and sign signifying you.

THE FOUND PICTURE

I

Flame and the garden we are together
In it using our secret time up.
We are together in this picture.

It is of the Early Italian School
And not great, a landscape
Maybe illustrating a fable.

We are those two figures barely
Discernible in the pool under
The umbra of the foreground tree.

Or that is how I see it. Nothing
Will move. This is a holy picture
Under its varnish darkening.

2

The Tree of Life unwraps its leaves
And makes its fruit like lightning.
Beyond the river the olive groves.

Beyond the olives musical sounds
Are heard. It is the old, authentic
Angels weeping out of bounds.

3

Observe how the two creatures turn
Slowly toward each other each
In the bare buff and yearning in

Their wordless place. The light years
Have over-varnished them to keep
Them still in their classic secrets.

I slant the canvas. Now look in
To where under the cracking black,
A third creature hides by the spring.

The painted face is faded with light
And the couple are aware of him.
They turn their tufts out of his sight

In this picture's language not
Wanting to be discovered. He
Is not a bad man or a caught

Tom peeping out of his true time.
He is a god making a funny
Face across the world's garden.

See they are fixed they cannot move
Within the landscape of our eyes.
What shall we say out of love

Turning toward each other to hide
In somewhere the breaking garden?
What shall we say to the hiding god?

IMPLEMENTS IN THEIR PLACES

1

Somewhere our belonging particles
Believe in us. If we could only find them.

2

Who calls? Don't fool me. Is it you
Or me or us in a faulty duet
Singing out of a glade in a wood
Which we would never really enter?

3

This time the muse in the guise
Of jailbait pressed against
That cheeky part of me which thinks
It likes to have its own way.
I put her out and made her change
Her coarse disguise but later she came
Into the room looking like an old
Tinopener and went to work on the company.

4

One night after punching the sexual
Clock I sat where I usually sit
Behind my barrier of propped words.
Who's there I shouted. And the face

Whitely flattened itself against
The black night-glass like a white pig
And entered and breathed beside me
Her rank breath of poet's bones.

5

When I was a buoy it seemed
Craft of rare tonnage
Moored to me. Now
Occasionally a skiff
Is tied to me and tugs
At the end of its tether.

6

He has been given a chair in that
Timeless University.
The Chair of Professor of Silence.

7

My father's ego sleeps in my bones
And wakens suddenly to find the son
With words dressed up to kill or at
The least maim for life another
Punter met in the betting yard.

8

He cocked his snoot, settled his cock,
Said goodbye darling to his darling,
Splurged on a taxi, recited the name
Of his host and wondered who would be there

Worthy of being his true self to.
They were out. It was the wrong night.
By underground he returned home
To his reading darling saying darling
Halfway there I realised the night
Would have been nothing without you there.

9

She stepped from the bath, interestedly
Dried herself not allowing herself
To feel or expect too much. She sat
Not naked doing her face thinking
I am a darling but what will they think
When I arrive without my darling.
Moving in her perfumed aura,
Her earrings making no sound,
She greets her hostess with a cheek-kiss
And dagger. Then disentangled
She babys her eyes and sends her gaze
Widening to wander through
The sipping archipelagoes
Of frantic islands. He was there
It was their night. Groomed again
She lets herself in at four with an oiled
Key thinking my handsome darling
Is better than me, able to pull
Our house and the children round him.

10

Out into across
The morning loch burnished
Between us goes the flat
Thrown poem and lands

Takes off and skips One
2, 3, 4, 5, 6, 7, 8, 9,
And ends and sinks under.

11

Mister Montgomerie. Mister Scop.
You, follicles. You, the owl.
Two famous men famous for far
Apart images. POLEEP POLEEP
The owl calls through the olive grove.
I come to her in a set-in bed
In a Greenock tenement. I see
The little circle of brown moles
Round her nipple. Good Montgomerie.

12

I could know you if I wanted to.
You make me not want to.
Why does everybody do that?

13

Down in a business well
In a canyon in lower Manhattan
I glanced up from the shades
To see old dye-haired Phoebus
Swerving appear in his gold
Souped-up convertible.

14

The greedy rooks. The Maw
Of the incongruous deep.

The appetite of the long
Barrelled gun of the sea.
The shrew's consumption.
And me abroad ahunting
Those distant morsels
Admired by man.

15

Raped by his colour slides her delighted
Pupils fondled their life together.
It was the fifty dirty milkbottles
Standing like an army turned their love sour.

16

Failures of love make their ghosts
Which float out from every object
The lovers respectively have ever
Sighed and been alive towards.

17

Sign me my right on the pillow of cloudy night.

18

In my task's husk a whisper said
Drop it It's bad It's bad anyhow.
Because I could not gracefully
Get out of what I was doing, I made
An inner task come to fruit
Invisible to all spectators.

19

The fine edge of the wave expects.
Ireland Scotland England expects.
He She They expect. My dear
Expects. And I am ready to see
How I should not expect to ever
Enfold her. But I do expect.

20

So sleeps and does not sleep
The little language of green glow
Worms by the wall where the mint sprouts.
The tails the tales of love are calling.

21

When you were younger and me hardly
Anything but who is in me still
I had a throat of loving for you
That I can hardly bear can bear.

22

I see it has fluttered to your hand
Drowned and singed. Can you read it?
It kills me. Why do you persist
In holding my message upsidedown?

23

Ho Ho Big West Prevailer,
Your beard brushes the gable
But tonight you make me sleep.

24

It is how one two three each word
Chose itself in its position
Pretending at the same time
They were working for me. Here
They are. Should I have sacked them?

25

At times a rare metaphor's
Fortuitous agents sing
Equally in their right.

26

Nouns are the very devil. Once
When the good nicely chosen verb
Came up which was to very do,
The king noun took the huff and changed
To represent another object.
I was embarrassed but I said something
Else and kept the extravert verb.

27

Only now a wordy ghost
Of once my firmer self I go
Floating across the frozen tundra
Of the lexicon and the dictionary.

28

Commuting by arterial words
Between my home and Cool Cat
Reality, I began to seem
To miss or not want to catch
My road to one or the other. Rimbaud
Knew what to do. Or Nansen letting
His world on the wooden Fram freeze in
To what was going to carry him.

29

These words as I uttered them
Spoke back at me out of spite,
Pretended to not know me
From Adam. Sad to have to infer
Such graft and treachery in the name
Of communication. O it's become
A circus of mountebanks, promiscuous
Highfliers, tantamount to wanting
To be servant to the more interesting angels.

30

Language, constrictor of my soul,
What are you snivelling at? Behave
Better. Take care. It's only through me
You live. Take care. Don't make me mad.

31

How are we doing not very well?
Perhaps the real message gets lost.
Or is it tampered with on the way
By the collective pain of Alive?

32

Member of Topside Jack's trades,
I tie my verse in a true reef
Fast for the purpose of joining.

33

Do not think you have to say
Anything back. But you do
Say something back which I
Hear by the way I speak to you.

34

As I hear so I speak so I am so I think
You must be. O Please Please No.

35

Language, you terrible surrounder
Of everything, what is the good
Of me isolating my few words
In a certain order to send them
Out in a suicide torpedo to hit?
I ride it. I will never know.

36

I movingly to you moving
Move on stillness I pretend
Is common ground forgetting not
Our sly irreconcilabilities.

Dammit these words are making faces
At me again. I hope the faces
They make at you have more love.

There must be a way to begin to try
Even to having to make up verse
Hoping that the poem's horned head
Looks up over the sad zoo railings
To roar whine bark in the characteristic
Gesture of its unique kind.
Come, my beast, there must be a way
To employ you as the whiskered Art
Object, or great Art-Eater
Licking your tongue into the hill.
The hunter in the language wood
Down wind is only after your skin.
Your food has stretched your neck too
Visible over the municipal hedge.
If I were you (which only I am)
I would not turn my high head
Even to me as your safe keeper.

Why should I hang around and yet
Whatever it is I want to say
Delays me. Am I greedier than you?
I linger on to hope to hear
The whale unsounding with a deep
Message about how I have behaved.
Down under in the indigo pressures
He counts the unsteady shriek of my pulse.

Kind me (O never never).
I leave you this space
To use as your own.
I think you will find
That using it is more
Impossible than making it.
Here is the space now.
Write an Implement in it.

YOU ....
YOU ....
YOU ....
YOU ....

Do it with your pen.
I will return in a moment
To see what you have done.
Try. Try. No offence meant.

41

I found her listed under Flora
Smudged on a coloured, shining plate
Dogeared and dirty. As for Fauna
We all are that, pelted with anarchy.

42

Your eyes glisten with wet spar.
My lamp dims in your breath. I want
I want out of this underword
But I can't turn round to crawl back.

43

Here now at the Poetry Face
My safety lamp names the muse Mineral.

44

Brushing off my hurts I came across
A thorn of Love deeply imbedded.
My wife lent me her eye-brow tweezers
And the little bad shaft emerged.
It is on the mantel-piece now but O
The ghost of the pain gives me gyp.

45

Tonight late alone, the only
Human awake in the house I go
Out in a foray into my mind
Armed with the language as I know it
To sword-dance in the halls of Angst.

46

By night a star-distinguisher
Looking up through the signed air.
By day an extinguisher of birds
Of silence caught in my impatient
Too-small-meshed poet's net.

47

Under his kilt his master
Led him to play the fool
Over the border and burn

A lady in her tower
In a loud lorry road
In tulipless Holland Park.

48

It is only when the tenant is gone
The shell speaks of the sea.

49

Knock knock. I knock on the drowned cabin
Boy's sea-chest. Yearning Corbiere
Eases up the lid to look out
And ask how is the sea today.

50

I dive to knock on the rusted, tight
Haspt locker of David Jones.
Who looks out? A mixed company.
Kandinsky's luminous worms,
Shelley, Crane and Melville and all
The rest. Who knows? Maybe even Eliot.

51

Hello. It's a pleasure. Is that a knowledge
You wear? You are dressed up today,
Brigit of early shallows of all
My early life wading in pools.
She lifts my words as a shell to hear
The Celtic wild waves learning English.

These words as they are (The beasts!)
Will never realise the upper
Hand is mine. They try to come
The tin-man with me. But now (I ask.)
Where do they think what do they think
They are now? The dear upstarts.

53

The word unblemished by the tongue
Of History has still to be got.
You see, Huntly, it is the way
You put it. Said Moray's Earl,
You've spoilt a bonnier face than your ain.
That's what he said when Huntly struck
The Scots iron into his face.

54

Officer myself, I had orders
To stay put, not to advance
On the enemy whose twigs of spring
Waved on their helmets as they less
Leadered than us deployed across
The other side of the ravine of silence.

55

From ventricle to ventricle
A sign of assumed love passes
To keep the organisation going.
Sometimes too hard sometimes too soft

I hear the night and the day mares
Galloping in the tenement top
In Greenock in my child brain.

56

Terrible the indignity of one's self flying
Away from the sleight of one's true hand.
Then it becomes me writing big
On the mirror and putting a moustache on myself.

57

There is no fifty-seven.
It is not here. Only
Freshwater Loch Thom
To paddle your feet in
And the long cry of the curlew.

58

Occasionally it is always night
Then who would hesitate to turn
To hope to see another face
Which is not one's own growing
Out of the heaving world's ship-wall?
From my bunk I prop myself
To look out through the salted glass
And see the school of black killers.
Grampus homes on the Graham tongue.

59

I've had enough said twig Ninety-thousand
Whispering across the swaying world
To twig Ninety-thousand-and-Fifty. This lack
Of communication takes all the sap
Out of me so far out. It is true.
They were on their own out at the edge
Changing their little live angles.
They were as much the tree as the trunk.
They were restless because the trunk
Seemed to never speak to them.
I think they were wrong. I carved my name
On the bark and went away hearing
The rustle of their high discussion.

60

I stand still and the wood marches
Towards me and divides towards
Me not to cover me up strangled
Under its ancient live anchors.
I stand in a ride now. And at
The meeting, dusk-filled end I see
(I wish I saw.) the shy move
Of the wood's god approaching to greet me.

61

You will observe that not one
Of those tree-trunks has our initials
Carved on it or heart or arrow
We could call ours. My dear, I think
We have come in to the wrong wood.

In Madron Wood the big cock rook
Says CHYUCK CHYUCK if I may speak
Here on behalf of our cock members,
This year we're building early and some
Of us have muses due to lay.

Feeding the dead is necessary.

I love you paralysed by me.
I love you made to lie. If you
Love me blink your right eye once.
If you don't love me blink your left.
Why do you flutter your just before
Dying dear two eyes at once?

Cretan girl in black, young early
Widow from stark Malia, please have
The last portion and let your mask
Go down on the handkerchief dancing floor.
It's me that's lost. Find me and put
Me into an octopus jar and let me
Be left for the young spectacled
Archaeologist sad in a distant womb.

66

I caught young Kipling in his pelmanic
Kimsgame scribbling on his cuff.
I found he was only counting the beasts
Of empire still abroad in the jungle.

67

Coming back to earth under my own
Name whispered by the under dear,
I extracted with care my dead right arm,
An urchin of pins and needles of love.

68

The earth was never flat. Always
The mind or earth wanderers' choice
Was up or down, a lonely vertical.

69

The long loch was not long enough.
The resident heron rose and went
That long length of water trailing
Its legs in air but couldn't make it.
He decided to stay then and devote
Himself to writing verse with his long
Beak in the shallows of the long loch-side.

70

(Is where you listen from becoming
Numb by the strike of the same key?)
It is our hazard. Heraklion, listen.

I can discern at a pinch you
Through the lens of the ouzo glass,
Your face globing this whole Piraeus
Taverna of buzzing plucked wires.
Here we are sitting, we two
In a very deep different country
At this table in the dark.
Inevitable tourists us,
Not in Scotland sitting here
In foreign shadows, bouzouki
Turning us into two others
Across the waiting eating table.
At home in Blantyre if your mother
Looked at the map with a microscope
Her Scotch palate would be appalled
To see us happy in the dark
Fishing the legs of creature eight
Out of the hot quink ink to eat.

72

I am not here. I am not here
At two o'clock in the morning just
For fun. I am not here for something.

73

Of air he knows nor does he speak
To earth. The day is sailing round
His heavenly wings. Daisies and cups
Of butter and dragonflies stop
Their meadow life to look up wondering
How out of what ridiculous season
The wingèd one descends.

Somewhere our belonging particles
Believe in us. If we could only find them.

DEAR BRYAN WYNTER

I

This is only a note
To say how sorry I am
You died. You will realise
What a position it puts
Me in. I couldn't really
Have died for you if so
I were inclined. The carn
Foxglove here on the wall
Outside your first house
Leans with me standing
In the Zennor wind.

Anyhow how are things?
Are you still somewhere
With your long legs
And twitching smile under
Your blue hat walking
Across a place? Or am
I greedy to make you up
Again out of memory?
Are you there at all?
I would like to think
You were all right
And not worried about
Monica and the children
And not unhappy or bored.

2

Speaking to you and not
Knowing if you are there
Is not too difficult.
My words are used to that.
Do you want anything?
Where shall I send something?
Rice-wine, meanders, paintings
By your contemporaries?
Or shall I send a kind
Of news of no time
Leaning against the wall
Outside your old house.

The house and the whole moor
Is flying in the mist.

3

I am up. I've washed
The front of my face
And here I stand looking
Out over the top
Half of my bedroom window.
There almost as far
As I can see I see
St Buryan's church tower.
An inch to the left, behind
That dark rise of woods,
Is where you used to lurk.

4

This is only a note
To say I am aware
You are not here. I find
It difficult to go
Beside Housman's star
Lit fences without you.
And nobody will laugh
At my jokes like you.

5

Bryan, I would be obliged
If you would scout things out
For me. Although I am not
Just ready to start out.
I am trying to be better,
Which will make you smile
Under your blue hat.

I know I make a symbol
Of the foxglove on the wall.
It is because it knows you.